To Mary Grace
My special friend &
"saleswoman Patty" We
love You.

Happy Birthday

To Joe, Mr Gary
Mr Patty, Jake & Scott
Ali Scott Jake & Scott

Enjoy this good book

Oct. 21, 2009

THE ADVENTURES OF
ROBIN HOOD

THE CLASSIC TALE

From the story by J. Walker McSpadden

Illustrated by Greg Hildebrandt

COURAGE BOOKS

AN IMPRINT OF RUNNING PRESS
PHILADELPHIA • LONDON

For information regarding print editions or original Hildebrandt art,
please contact Spiderwebart Gallery, 973 770 8189 or
go to http://www.spiderwebart.com.

9   8   7   6   5   4   3   2   1
Digit on the right indicates the number of this printing

Library of Congress Cataloging-in-Publication Number 2004109283
ISBN 0-7624-2197-5

Cover illustration by Greg Hildebrandt
Cover and Interior Design by Frances J. Soo Ping Chow
Typography: Bembo and Perpetua
Text adapted and abridged by Christopher Stella

This book may be ordered by mail from the publisher.
But try your bookstore first!

Published by Courage Books, an imprint of
Running Press Book Publishers
125 South Twenty-second Street
Philadelphia, Pennsylvania 19103-4399

Visit us on the web!
www.runningpress.com

In the days of good King Harry the Second of England there were forests in the North Country set aside for the King's hunting. These forests were guarded by the King's Foresters. One of the greatest of royal preserves was Sherwood Forest near Nottingham. Here dwelt Hugh Fitzooth as Head Forester, with his good wife, and son Robert. The boy had been born in Lockesley town and was often called Lockesley, or Rob of Lockesley. As soon as he was old enough, Rob learned to draw the long bow and speed a true arrow.

Two playmates had Rob. One was Will Gamewell, his cousin. The other was Marian Fitzwalter. Rob's father and Marian's father were enemies, but little cared Rob or Marian for this enmity.

Rob's father had two other enemies besides Fitzwalter in the lean Sheriff of Nottingham and the fat Bishop of Hereford. These three enemies one day got possession of the King's ear and whispered therein to such good—or evil—purpose that Hugh Fitzooth was removed from his post and the Sheriff arrested the Forester for treason and carried him to Nottingham jail. Rob and his mother turned for succor to their only kinsman, Squire George of Gamewell, who sheltered them in all kindness.

But the shock proved too much for Dame Fitzooth. In less than two months, she was no more. Rob met another crushing blow in the loss of his father, who died in prison.

Two years passed by. Rob's cousin Will was away at school; and Marian's father had sent his daughter to the court of Queen Eleanor. So these years were lonely ones to the orphaned lad.

One morning as Rob came in to breakfast, his uncle greeted

him with, "I have news for you! The Fair is on at Nottingham, and the Sheriff proclaims an archer's tournament. The one who shoots straightest of all will win a golden arrow."

"I should dearly love to let arrow fly alongside another man," answered Rob. "And a place among the Foresters is what I have long desired." So the young man set about making preparations for the journey.

A few days after, Rob was seen passing by way of Lockesley through Sherwood Forest to Nottingham town. Briskly walked he and gaily, for his hopes were high and never an enemy had he in the wide world, when he came suddenly upon a group of Foresters. One of them was the man who had taken his father's place as Head Forester. This man bellowed out: "Where go you, with that tupenny bow and toy arrows?"

"My bow is as good as yours," Rob retorted. "And my shafts will carry as straight and as far. So I'll not take lessons of any of you."

"Show us some of your skill, and if you can hit the mark here's twenty silver pennies for you," answered the leader. He pointed to a herd of deer distant a full five-score yards. "If your young arm could speed a shaft for half that distance, I'd shoot with you."

"Done!" cried Rob. And without more ado the shaft whistled across the glade. Another moment and the leader of the herd leaped high in his tracks and fell prone.

A murmur of amazement swept through the Foresters, and then a growl of rage. He that had wagered was angriest of all. "You have killed a King's deer," he cried. "Get ye gone straight, and let me not look upon your face again."

Rob's blood boiled within him. "I have looked upon your face once too often already. 'Tis you who wear my father's shoes."

The Forester, red with rage, seized his bow, strung an arrow, and without warning launched it full at Rob. The arrow whizzed by his ear. Rob turned upon his assailant, "Ha!" said he. "You shoot not so straight as I. Take this from the tupenny bow!" Straight flew his answering shaft. The Head Forester gave one cry, then fell face downward and lay still. His life had avenged Rob's father, but the son was now an outlaw. Forward he ran through the forest, before the band could gather their wits.

Toward the close of the same day, Rob paused hungry and weary at the cottage of a poor widow who dwelt upon the outskirts of the forest.

"'Tis an evil wind that blows through Sherwood," she said. "The poor are despoiled and the rich ride over their bodies. My three sons have been outlawed for shooting King's deer to keep us from starving, and now hide in the wood."

"Where are they?" cried Rob. "By my faith, I will join them."

"My sons will visit me tonight. Stay and see them if you must."

So Rob stayed willingly to see the widow's sons that night. One of them said, "We have agreed that he who has skill enough to go to Nottingham and win the prize at archery shall be our chief."

Rob sprang to his feet. "Said in good time!" cried he. "For I had started to that same fair, and all the Sheriff's men shall not stand between me and the center of their target!" And he stood so straight and his eye flashed with such fire that the three brothers seized his hand and shouted: "A Lockesley! A Lockesley! If you win the golden arrow you shall be chief of outlaws in Sherwood Forest!"

So Rob fell to planning how he could disguise himself, for he knew that the Foresters had even then set a price on his head.

The great event of the day came in the afternoon. It was the archer's contest for the golden arrow. Twenty men stepped forth to shoot. A great crowd had assembled in the amphitheater. The central box contained the pompous Sheriff, his wife, and their daughter who was hoping to receive the golden arrow from the victor.

On the other side was a box wherein sat a girl whose fair features caused Rob's heart to leap. 'Twas Maid Marian!

The trumpet sounded, the herald announced the terms of the contest, and the archers prepared to shoot. Rob shot sixth in the line and landed fairly, being rewarded by an approving grunt from the man with the green blinder, who shot seventh.

The trumpet sounded again, and a new target was set up. Rob fitted his arrow quietly and sped it unerringly toward the shining circle. The other archers in this round missed one after another and dropped moodily back. And now the herald summoned Rob to the Sheriff's box to receive the prize.

"You are a curious fellow enough," said the Sheriff, "yet you shoot well. What name go you by?"

"I am called Rob the Stroller, my Lord Sheriff," said the archer.

"Rob the Stroller," said he, "here is the golden arrow. See that you bestow it worthily."

At this point the herald nudged Rob and half inclined his head toward the Sheriff's daughter. But Rob took the arrow and

strode to the box where sat Maid Marian. "Lady," he said, "pray accept this little pledge from a poor stroller."

"My thanks to you, Rob in the Hood," she replied with a twinkle in her eye.

The Sheriff glowered furiously upon this ragged archer who had taken his prize without a word of thanks and snubbed his daughter. But Rob had already headed straight for the town gate.

That same evening within a forest glade a group of men—some two-score clad in Lincoln green—sat round a fire making merry.

"I look for the widow's sons," a clear voice said.

"'Tis Rob!" they cried. Then one of the widow's sons, Stout Will, stepped forth and said: "Comrades, you know that our band has lacked a leader. Be like we have found that leader in this young man. I and my brothers have told him that the band would choose that one who should bring the Sheriff to shame this day and capture his golden arrow. Is it not so?"

The band gave assent.

Rob laughed. "In truth, I brought the Sheriff to shame. But as to the prize you must take my word, for I bestowed it upon a maid."

The men stood in doubt at this. Then stepped one forward from the rest, a tall swarthy man. And Rob recognized him as the man with the green blinder.

"Rob in the Hood—for such the lady called you," said he. "I can vouch for your tale." Good Will Stutely told the outlaws of Rob's deeds and the other members hailed him as their leader, by the name of Robin Hood.

They gave Robin Hood a horn upon which he was to blow to summon them. They swore, also, that while they might take money and goods from the unjust rich, they would aid and befriend the poor and the helpless.

How Robin Hood Met
Little John

ALL THAT SUMMER, Robin Hood and his merry men roamed Sherwood Forest and the fame of their deeds ran abroad in the land. The band increased till four-score good men had sworn fealty.

But the days of quiet grew irksome to Robin's adventurous spirit. Up rose he one morn, slung his quiver over his shoulders, and strode merrily forward to the edge of the wood. The highway led clear in the direction of town, but at a bend in the road he knew of a path leading across a brook which made the way nearer. The log foot-bridge was there but he was no sooner started across than he saw a tall stranger coming from the other side. Midway they met, and neither would yield an inch.

"Give way, fellow!" roared Robin.

The stranger smiled. He was almost a head taller than Rob. "Nay," he retorted. "I give way only to a better man than myself."

"Give way," repeated Robin, "or I shall have to show you a better man."

His opponent laughed loudly. "Show him to me."

"That will I right soon," quoth Robin. "Stay you here a little while till I cut me a cudgel like unto that you have been twiddling in your fingers." So saying, he sought his own bank and cut himself

12

a stout staff of oak. Then back came he boldly. Here he whirred the staff about his head by way of practice. "Have at you!"

Whack! whack! whack! whack!

The fight waxed fast and furious and the match was a merry one. Each stood firmly in his place not moving backward or forward for a good half hour. The giant stepped forth with a furious onslaught. Robin sprang in swiftly and unexpectedly and dealt the stranger a blow upon the short ribs.

"By my life, you can hit hard!" gasped the giant, giving back a blow. It caught Robin off his guard and forthwith he dropped neatly into the stream.

The giant could not forbear laughing heartily at his plight, but also thrust down his long staff to Robin. Robin laid hold and was hauled to dry land like a fish.

"By all the saints!" said he, "My head hums like a hive of bees." Then he seized his horn and blew three shrill notes. Forth from the glade burst a score of stalwart yeomen with good Will Stutely at their head.

"Good master," cried Will Stutely, "there is not a dry thread on your body."

"This fellow would not let me pass the footbridge and when I tickled him in the ribs, he answered by a pat on the head which landed me overboard," replied Robin.

"I would like to know your name," the other man said to Robin.

"My men and even the Sheriff of Nottingham know me as Robin Hood. You have not yet told us your name," said Robin.

"Whence I came, men call me John Little."

"Enter our company then, John Little."

Thereupon Will Stutely, who loved a good jest, spoke up and said: "This fair little stranger is so small that his old name is not to the purpose. My son, take your new name on entering the forest. I christen you Little John."

How Robin Hood Met
Will Scarlet

ONE FINE MORNING SOMETIME LATER, Robin Hood and Little John went strolling through the wood. They directed their steps to the brook to quench their thirst and rest in the cool bushes. Presently they heard someone coming up the road whistling gaily. In a minute more, up came a smart stranger dressed in scarlet and silk. His hair was long and yellow and a goodly sword hung at his side.

Little John clucked his teeth at this sight. "Not so bad a build for all his prettiness."

"Nay," retorted Robin. "He would run and bellow lustily at the sight of a quarter-staff. Stay you behind this bush."

So saying, Robin Hood stepped forth briskly and planted himself in the way of the scarlet stranger. "Hold!" quoth the outlaw.

"And who may you be?" asked the other coolly.

"What my name is matters not," said Robin. "But know that I am an equalizer of shillings. Hand over your purse."

The other smiled sweetly. "I am deeply sorrowful that I cannot show my purse to every rough lout that asks to see it. Pray stand aside."

"Nay, that will I not!" quoth Robin hotly. And he swung his quarter-staff threateningly.

"Alas!" moaned the stranger shaking his head. "Now I shall have to run this fellow through with my sword." He drew his shining blade.

"Put by your weapon," said Robin. "Get you a stick like mine and we will fight fairly."

The stranger laid the sword aside and walked over to the oak thicket. He found a stout little tree to his liking and gave a tug. Up it came root and all, and the stranger walked back trimming it as though pulling up trees were the easiest thing in the world.

Robin put his oak staff at parry as the other took his stand. Back and forth swayed the fighters, their cudgels pounding this way and that. Twice did the scarlet man smite Robin. The first well nigh broke Robin's fingers. And while he was dancing about in pain, the other's staff came swinging through at one side—zip!—and struck him under the arm. Down went Robin into the dust of the road.

"Hold!" said Little John, bursting out of the bushes and seizing the stranger's weapon.

The stranger had been eyeing Robin attentively. "If I mistake not," he said at last, "you are Robin Hood."

"You say right," replied Robin.

"Now why did I not know you at once?" continued the stranger. "Do you know me, Rob? Have you ever been to Gamewell Lodge?"

"Will Gamewell!" shouted Robin, throwing his arms about the other in sheer affection.

Will embraced his cousin no less heartily.

"But why seek you me?" asked Robin.

"'Twas for my father's sake that I am now an outlaw like yourself. He had a steward who boot-licked his way to favor until he lorded it over the whole house. One day I smote him a blow mightier than I intended. The fellow rolled over and never breathed afterwards. Is this Little John the Great? Promise to cross a staff with me in friendly bout some day!"

"That will I!" quoth Little John heartily. "What is your last name again, say you?"

"'Tis to be changed," interposed Robin. "In scarlet he came to us, and that shall be his name henceforth!"

How Robin Hood Met Friar Tuck

ONE DAY AFTER A PRACTICE at shooting in which Little John struck down a hart at five hundred feet distance, Robin Hood took to boasting of his own skill.

Will Scarlet laughed. "There lives a friar in Fountain's Abbey—Tuck, by name—who can beat both him and you," he said.

Robin pricked up his ears. "By our Lady," he said, "I'll neither eat nor drink till I see this friar." He at once set about arming himself for the adventure. Underneath his Lincoln green he wore a coat of chain metal. Then, with sword and buckler girded at his side, his stout yew bow and a sheaf of chosen arrows, he set forth upon his way. Steadily he pressed forward till he came to a green broad pasture at whose edge flowed a stream. Robin did not fancy getting

his fine suit of mail rusted so he paused on the hither bank. As he sat down he heard snatches of a jovial song floating to him from the farther side.

The willows parted on the other bank. It was a stout friar. In his hand was a huge pasty pie. Robin seized his bow and fitted a shaft.

"Hey, friar!" he sang out. "Carry me over the water or else I cannot answer for your safety."

"Put down your bow," the friar shouted back, "and I will bring you over the brook." So the friar laid aside his pie and his cloak and his sword and waded across the stream. Then he took Robin Hood upon his back to the other side.

Lightly leaped Robin off his back, and said, "I am much beholden to you."

"Beholden say you!" rejoined the other, drawing his sword. "Then shall you repay your score. In short, you must carry me back again."

Robin took him up. The fat friar hung on and dug his heels into his steed's ribs, while as for poor Robin, he gasped like the winded horse he was. At last he managed to stagger out on the bank.

No sooner had he set the friar down than he seized his own sword. "Now, holy friar," quoth he, "You must carry me back again or I swear that I will make a cheese-cloth out of your jacket!"

So Robin mounted again and carried his sword in his hand. But he felt himself slipping from the friar's back. Down went he with a loud splash into the middle of the stream.

"There!" quoth the holy man. And he gained his own bank,

while Robin thrashed about until he made shift to grasp a willow wand and thus haul himself ashore on the other side.

"You bloody villain!" shouted Robin.

"Soft you and fair!" said the friar unconcernedly. "Meet me halfway in the stream." The friar waded into the brook, sword in hand, where he was met halfway by the impetuous outlaw. Thereupon began a fierce and mighty battle. Many a smart blow was landed but each wore an undercoat of linked mail which might not be pierced. Once and again they paused by mutual consent and caught breath.

Robin Hood set his horn to mouth, blew mighty blasts, and half a hundred yeomen came raking over the lee.

"Friar Tuck!" shouted Will Scarlet, who stood laughing heartily at the scene.

"Friar Tuck!" exclaimed Robin, astounded. "You are he I came to seek."

"I am but a poor friar," said the other, "by name Friar Tuck. I would like to know you."

"'Tis Robin Hood," said Will Scarlet.

Replied Robin gaily, "Will you not join our band?"

"That will I!" cried Friar Tuck jovially

How Allan-A-Dale's Wooing
Was Prospered

S o Robin walked forth into the wood that evening in great contentment. He stepped behind a tree when he heard a man's voice in song.

This fellow was clad in scarlet. He bore a harp in his hand, which he thrummed while his lusty tenor voice rang out.

Robin let the singer pass and went back to his camp, where he told of the minstrel. "If any of ye set on him after this," quoth he in ending, "bring him to me, for I would have speech with him."

The very next day, Little John and Much the miller's son spied the same young man; at least, they thought it must be he, for he was clad in scarlet and carried a harp in his hand. But now his scarlet was all in tatters and at every step he fetched a sigh.

No sooner did the young man catch sight of them than he bent his bow and held an arrow back to his ear.

"Put by your weapon," said Much. "We will not harm you. But you must come before our master straight." So the minstrel put by his bow and suffered himself to be led before Robin Hood.

"How now!" quoth Robin. "Are you not he whom I heard yesternight caroling so blithely?"

"The same in body, sir," replied the other sadly. "But my spirit is grievously changed. Yesterday I stood pledged to a maid. But she is to become an old knight's bride this very day. Her brother says she shall wed a title, and he and the old knight have fixed it up for today."

"What is your name?" asked Robin Hood.

"By the faith of my body," replied the young man, "my name is Allan-a-Dale. If you give me back my love, I will be your true servant forever after."

"Where is this wedding to take place, and when?" asked Robin.

"At Plympton Church, at three o' the afternoon."

"Then to Plympton we will go!" cried Robin.

The fat Bishop of Hereford was full of pomp and importance that day at Plympton Church. Already were the guests beginning to assemble when the Bishop saw a minstrel clad in green walk up boldly to the door and peer within. It was Robin Hood, who had borrowed Allan's be-ribboned harp.

"Now who are you, fellow?" quoth the Bishop.

Robin bowed humbly. "I am a harper, the best in the whole North Country."

"Then welcome, good minstrel," said the Bishop. "Here comes the party now."

Then up the lane to the church came the old knight, preceded by ten archers. Their master walked slowly, leaning upon a cane. And after them came a sweet lass leaning upon her brother's arm. She had been weeping.

"Now strike up your music, fellow!" ordered the Bishop.

"Right gladly will I," quoth Robin. And he drew forth his bugle from underneath his cloak and blew three winding notes.

"Seize him!" yelled the Bishop. "These are the tricks of Robin Hood!"

The ten archers rushed forward from the rear of the church, but their rush was blocked by the onlookers who now crowded the aisles. Meanwhile Robin had stationed himself by the altar. "Stand where you are!" he shouted, drawing his bow. "All ye who have come to witness a wedding stay in your seats. We shall have one."

Then four-and-twenty good bowmen came marching in

with Will Stutely at their head. And they seized the ten archers and the bride's brother and the other men on guard and bound them prisoners.

Then in came Allan-a-Dale. The maiden smiled and clasped her arms about his neck. "That is her true love," said Robin. "Good friar, bless this pair with book and candle."

So Friar Tuck came forward and began with the ceremony and the twain were declared man and wife.

How The Widow's Three Sons Were Rescued

THE WEDDING PARTY WAS A MERRY ONE that left Plympton Church, but not so merry were the ones left behind. It was not until the next day that they were released. The Bishop and the old knight made straight to Nottingham and levied the Sheriff's forces.

A hundred picked men from the Royal Foresters, and swordsmen of the shire gathered together and marched straightway into the greenwood. There, they surprised some score of outlaws hunting and instantly gave chase.

One outlaw in his flight stumbled and fell. Two others instantly stopped and helped to put him on his feet again. They were the widow's three sons, Stout Will, Lester, and John. The party of Sheriff's men got above them and cut them off from their fellows. Then they bound the widow's three sons and carried them back to Nottingham.

Robin Hood, returning to the camp, was met by the widow herself. "Master Robin!" said the dame wildly. "God keep ye from the fate that has met my three sons! The Sheriff has them and they are condemned to die."

Then Robin Hood sped straightway to the forest camp, where he heard the details of the skirmish.

"We must rescue them!" quoth Robin, and the band set to work to devise ways and means.

Robin walked apart a little when whom should he meet but an old begging palmer. Then Robin's idea came to him like a flash. "Come, change thine apparel with me, old man," he said, "and I'll give thee forty shillings in good silver."

So the palmer was persuaded, and Robin put on the old man's hat and his cloak.

The next morning the whole town of Nottingham was early astir. Robin Hood, in his palmer's disguise, entered the gates. Presently he came to the marketplace, where the Sheriff stalked pompously up to inspect the gallows.

"O, Heaven save you, worshipful Sheriff!" said the palmer. "What will you give a silly old man to be your hangman? I can shrive their souls and hang their bodies most devoutly."

"Very good," replied the other. "The fee today is thirteen pence."

"God bless ye!" said the palmer.

Just before the stroke of noon, the doors of the prison opened and the procession of the condemned came forth. At the gallows they halted, and the three men, with arms bound tightly behind their backs, ascended the scaffold.

Then Robin stepped to the edge of the scaffold, and forth

from the robe he drew his horn and blew three loud blasts thereon. His keen hunting-knife flew forth and in a trice, Stout Will, Lester, and merry John were free.

"Seize them! 'Tis Robin Hood!" screamed the Sheriff, "an hundred pounds if ye hold them, dead or alive!"

"I make it two hundred!" roared the fat Bishop.

But their voices were drowned in the uproar that ensued. Down through the crowd rushed four-score men in Lincoln green. With swords drawn they fell upon the guard from every side at once. The gate was reached, and the long road leading up the hill, and at last the protecting greenwood itself.

How Robin Hood Came Before
Queen Eleanor

Now it fell out that Robin was minded to try his skill at hunting. Not knowing whom he might meet, he stained his face and put on a long cloak. Presently a hart entered the glade in full view of him. Suddenly, the beast fell, pierced by a clever arrow from the far side of the glade. A little page sprang gleefully from the covert and ran toward the dying animal. This was plainly the archer.

Robin approached the hart from the other side.

"Who are you, my lad?" Robin said civilly.

"No lad of yours," retorted the other with spirit.

"We of the forest will have to teach you manners!" said Robin.

"Not if *you* stand for the forest!" cried the page, whipping out his sword. Robin saw nothing for it but to draw likewise. The page thereupon engaged him quite fiercely. The fight lasted for above a quarter of an hour, at the end of which the outlaw allowed himself to be pricked slightly on the wrist.

"Are you satisfied, fellow?" asked the page.

"Aye," replied Robin. "To whom do I owe this scratch?"

"I am Richard Partington, page to Queen Eleanor," answered the lad with dignity while wiping his sword with a small lace kerchief. "I seek one Robin Hood, to whom I bring amnesty from the Queen." He replaced the kerchief in his shirt. As he did so, the gleam of a golden trophy caught the outlaw's eye.

Robin started forward with a joyful cry. "Ah! I know you now! By the sight of yon golden arrow, you are Maid Marian!"

"You—are—?" gasped Marian, for it was she; "not Robin!"

"Robin's self!" said he gaily. And forthwith, clasped the dainty page close to his breast.

She told him, as they walked back through the glade, that the fame of his prowess had reached Queen Eleanor's ears. And the Queen had promised him amnesty if he and four of his archers would repair to London for the next tournament to shoot against King Henry's picked men. Marian added: "The Queen bade me go, and sent this gold ring to you in token of her faith."

Robin took the ring and kissed it loyally. By this time they were come to the grove before the cave, and Robin presented Maid Marian to the band. That evening Robin bade Marian repeat her message from the Queen.

"Ye have heard," quoth Robin standing forth, "how Her Majesty wishes but four men to go with me. I choose Little John and Will Stutely, Will Scarlet, and Allan-a-Dale. We will depart with

"Thou art welcome, Lockesley," said the Queen smiling graciously.

early morning, decked in our finest.

The journey to London town was made without incident. So on they sped and in due course came to the palace itself to await audience with the Queen.

The Queen sat in her private audience-room chatting pleasantly with her ladies, when in came Mistress Marian Fitzwalter. Marian gave orders to a herald, and presently Robin Hood and his little party entered the room.

Robin advanced and knelt down before the Queen, and said: "Here I am, Robin Hood—I and my chosen men! I come bearing the ring of amnesty which I will protect—as I would protect Your Majesty's honor—with my life!"

"Thou art welcome, Lockesley," said the Queen smiling graciously.

Then Robin presented each of his men in turn, and each fell on his knee and was greeted with most kindly words. Then, at the Queen's request, they related to her and her ladies some of their merry adventures, whereat the listeners were vastly entertained, and laughed heartily.

How the Outlaws Shot in King Harry's Tourney

THE MORNING OF THE GREAT ARCHERY contest dawned fair and bright. The uprising tiers of seats filled early. The King and Queen ascended the steps of the royal box and seated themselves upon two thrones.

"Think you that your ten chosen fellows are the best bowmen

in all England?" asked the Queen.

"Aye," answered the King. "Thereunto I would stake five hundred pounds."

"If I produce five archers who can out-shoot your ten, will you grant my men full grace and amnesty?"

"Assuredly!" said the King, laughing. "How say you, if first we decide this open target and then match the five best thereat against your unknown champions?"

"Agreed," said the Queen.

Now the ten chosen archers from the King's bands came forth and took their stand. Gilbert of the White Hand led the shooting, and Tepus tied his score. The herald then came forward and proclaimed that there was to be a final contest. Two men had tied for first place, and three others were entitled to honors. Now all these five were to be pitted against five others of the Queen's choosing.

The gate at the far end of the field opened and five men entered. The leader was dressed in a brave suit of scarlet red. Up came the Bishop of Hereford.

"My liege lord!" cried he. "Yon man in scarlet is none other than Robin Hood himself. The others are all famous in the North Country for their deeds of violence."

The King's brows grew dark. "Is this true?" he demanded.

"Aye, my lord," responded the Queen demurely. "But I have your royal promise of grace and amnesty."

"That will I keep," said the King. "But only forty days do I grant of respite."

THE KING'S BROWS GREW DARK. "IS THIS TRUE?" HE DEMANDED.

A target was now set up and Clifton was bidden to shoot first. Will Scarlet was chosen to follow him. Each struck upon the bull's-eye. The target was then cleared for Geoffrey. Each of his shots allowed an easy space for Allan to graze within.

Robin broke off two straws and held them out. "The long straw goes next!" he decided, and it fell to Stutely. Elwyn was to precede him and his score was no whit better than Geoffrey's. Will loosed his shaft. It struck in the exact center.

Tepus was chosen to go next, placing his third in the center. Little John seemed determined to outdo Tepus by a tiny margin; his own shaft descended from above upon Tepus's final center shaft with a blow that drove the other out and left the outlaw's in its place. The King could scarce believe his eyes.

Gilbert now took his stand and shot his arrows into the bull's-eye. "Well done!" spoke up Robin Hood. "Now if you had placed one of your shafts *there*"—loosing one of his own—"and another *there*"—out sped the second—"and another *there*"—the third was launched—"mayhap the King would have declared you the best bowman in all England!"

His first two shafts had packed themselves into the small space left at the bull's-eye; while his third had split down between them.

Up rose the King in amazement and anger. "Gilbert is not beaten!" he cried. "Did he not shoot within the mark thrice?"

Robin bowed low. "Your Majesty!" quoth he. "May I be allowed to place the mark for the second shooting?"

The King waved his hand sullenly. Thereupon Robin got a

light, peeled willow wand which he set in the ground in place of the target.

"I can scarce see it," said Gilbert. His shaft flew harmlessly by the thin white streak. Then came Robin to his stand again. He let the feathered missile fly. The willow wand was split in twain.

Meanwhile the King had risen, signaling the judges to distribute the prizes.

Then the Queen beckoned the outlaws to approach. "Right well have ye served me," she said. "The King's word and grace hold true. As to these prizes ye have gained, I add the wagers I have won from His Majesty the King. Buy the best swords ye can find in London for all your band and swear with them to protect all the poor."

"We swear," said the five yeomen solemnly.

How Robin Hood Was Sought
Of the Tinker

King Henry was as good as his word, and for forty days no hand was raised against them. But at the end of that time, word was sent to the Sheriff at Nottingham that he must lay hold upon the outlaws.

Now the Sheriff's daughter had hated Robin Hood bitterly ever since the day he refused to bestow upon her the golden arrow. So she sought to aid the Sheriff in catching the enemy.

There came to the Mansion House a strolling tinker named Middle, a great braggart. He talked loudly about what *he* would do if he once came within reach of Robin Hood. The Sheriff's daughter called him to her. "I am minded to try your skill at outlaw

catching," she said. The tinker grinned broadly.

"Here is a warrant made out this morning by the Sheriff himself. See that you keep it safely," she told him.

Middle took the warrant and proceeded toward Sherwood. Soon he met a young man with curling brown hair and merry eyes. The newcomer accosted him.

"Good-day to you!" said he. "Whence come you?"

"I come from over against Banbury. I am especially commissioned to seek Robin Hood. I have a warrant from the Sheriff to take him where I can. If you can tell me where he is, I will make a man of you."

"The middle of the road on a hot July day is not a good place to talk things over," said the young man. "Let's go back to the inn and quench our thirst."

So back turned the tinker with the stranger and proceeded to the Inn of the Seven Does. The tinker asked for wine, and the young man, Robin in disguise, for ale. They lingered long over their cups, Master Middle emptying one after another while his companion expounded on the best plans for capturing Robin Hood. In the end the tinker fell sound asleep.

Then the stranger deftly opened the snoring man's pouch, took out the warrant and put it in his own wallet. Calling the host to him, he told him that the tinker would pay when he awoke.

Presently the tinker came to himself. "What were you saying, friend, about the best plan for catching this fellow? Where's the man gone? Host! Host!" he shouted, "where is that fellow? Help! Help! I've been robbed!"

"Cease your bellowing!" said the landlord. "What did you lose?"

"I had with me a warrant, granted under the hand of my lord High Sheriff of Nottingham, for the capture and arrest of Robin Hood."

Said the host, "Was he not with you in all good fellowship?"

" *That* was Robin Hood?" gasped Middle.

"Pay me the score for both of you," said the host.

"Take here my working-bag and my good hammer too," said Middle.

"Give me your leather coat as well," said the host, "and get you gone."

How Robin Hood
Met Sir Richard of the Lea

KING HENRY PASSED AWAY, and Richard of the Lion Heart was proclaimed as his successor. The new king had formerly set forth upon a crusade, and Prince John, his brother, was cruel and treacherous.

One morning in early autumn, Robin was walking along the edge of a small open glade busy with his thoughts. Presently a stag, wild and furious, dashed suddenly forth from among the trees. He saw the stag veer about and fix its gaze on the bushes to the left side of the glade. These were parted by a delicate hand, and through the opening appeared the slight figure of Maid Marian!

The beast rushed at this new and inviting target. A side blow from its antlers stretched her upon the ground. Then the shaft from Robin's bow went whizzing close above her head and struck full in the center of the stag's forehead. The beast fell dead across the body of the maid.

Robin quickly dragged the beast off the girl.

"Oh, Robin, it is you!" she murmured.

"Aye, 'tis I. I swear that I will not let you from my care henceforth."

Marian then told him how the Prince had seized upon her father's lands.

While Robin and Marian were having their encounter with the stag, Little John, Much, and Will Scarlet had sallied forth to watch the highroad when they spied a knight riding by in a very forlorn and careless manner. Little John came up to the knight and prayed him to accept the hospitality of the forest.

In the same lackadaisical fashion which had marked all his actions that day, the knight suffered his horse to be led to the rendezvous of the band in the greenwood.

"Welcome, Sir Knight," said Robin, courteously. "You are come in good time, for we were just preparing to sit down to meat."

After eating heartily, the knight brightened.

"Pledge me, Sir Knight!" cried the merry outlaw. "I see that your armor is bent and that your clothes are torn. Be not bashful with us."

The sorrowful guest replied, "My name is Sir Richard of the Lea. I went upon a crusade, from which I am but lately returned, in time to find my son grown up. But about this time he did accidentally kill a knight in the open lists. To save the boy, I had to sell my lands, and this not being enough, I have had to borrow money at a

"Welcome, Sir Knight," said Robin, courteously.

ruinous interest from my lord of Hereford."

"What is the sum of your debt?" asked Robin.

"Four hundred pounds," said Sir Richard.

Thereupon Little John and Will Scarlet went into the cave near by and returned bearing a bag of gold. There were four times one hundred gold pieces in it.

"Take this loan from us and pay your debt," said Robin.

The knight was sorrowful no longer. And after spending the night in rest, he mounted his steed the following morning an altogether different man.

"We shall wait for you in this place," said Robin, "and then you will repay us the loan, if you have been prosperous."

"I shall return it to you within the year, upon my honor." So saying, the knight rode down the forest glade till he was lost to view.

How The Sheriff Held Another Shooting Match

THE SHERIFF WENT TO LONDON TOWN to lay his troubles before the King. Prince John heard him with scorn. "Never let me see thy face at court again until thou hast a better tale to tell," said the Prince.

So away went the Sheriff in sorrier pass than ever. His daughter met him on his return.

"I have it!" she exclaimed at length. "Why should we not hold another shooting match? Belike Robin Hood's men will be tempted."

The Sheriff lost no time in proclaiming a tourney. It was open to all comers. Furthermore, an arrow with a golden head and shaft of silver-white should be given to the winner.

These tidings came to Robin Hood and fired his impetuous spirit. "Come, prepare ye," quoth he, "and we'll go to the Fair."

With that stepped forth the merry David of Doncaster. "Master," quoth he, "yon match is a trap."

"That," replied Robin, "pleases me not. Let come what will."

Maid Marian and Mistress Dale prepared some costumes and fitted out the seven-score men till you would never have taken them for other than villagers. And in through the gates trooped the whole company.

The herald now set forth the terms of the contest and the shooting presently began. Robin had chosen five of his men to shoot with him and the rest were to watch the gates. These five were Little John, Will Scarlet, Will Stutely, Much, and Allan-a-Dale.

Robin's men had done so well that the air was filled with shouts. Robin exchanged no word with his men, each treating the other as a stranger. Nonetheless, such great shooting could not pass without revealing the archers. The Sheriff discovered in the winner of the golden arrow, the person of Robin Hood. So he sent word privately for his men-at-arms to close round the group.

As Robin received his prize the Sheriff grasped him about the neck. But the moment the Sheriff touched Robin, he received such a buffet on the side of his head that he let go instantly.

By this time the conflict had become general, but the Sheriff's men suffered the disadvantage of being hampered by the crowd of innocent on-lookers.

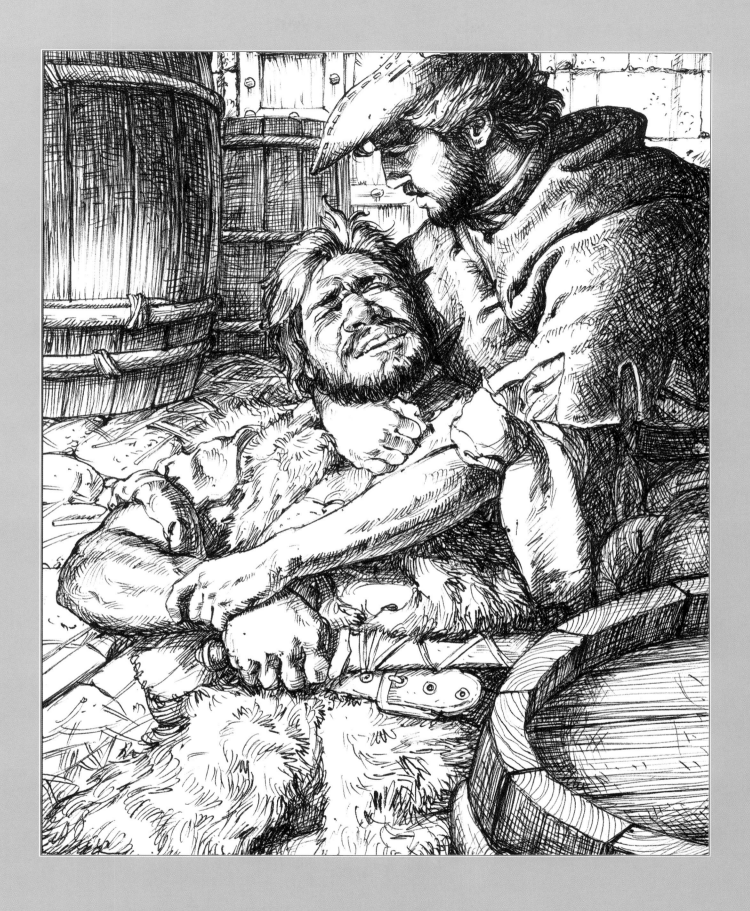

LITTLE JOHN SUDDENLY FELL FORWARD WITH A SLIGHT MOAN.

The clear bugle note from Robin ordered a retreat and out through the gate went the foresters in good order.

The soldiery pressed closely after the retreating outlaws. Then Little John suddenly fell forward with a slight moan. An arrow had pierced his knee. Robin seized the big fellow with almost superhuman strength. Up he took him on his back. He soon brought him within the shelter of the forest.

Once there, the Sheriff's men did not follow, and Robin caused a litter of boughs to be made for the wounded man. They carried him through the wood until the hermitage of Friar Tuck was reached, where his wounds were dressed.

It was found that Will Stutely was missing. Robin was seized with dread. The Sheriff would hang Will speedily if he were captured.

That evening, the Sheriff boasted of how he would make an example of the captured outlaw; for Stutely had indeed fallen into his hands. As he spoke a missive sped through a window and fell clattering upon his plate. It was the golden arrow and on it was sewed a little note which read:

"This from one who will take no gifts from liars and who henceforth will show no mercy. Look well to yourself. R.H."

How Will Stutely Was Rescued

THE NEXT DAY ROBIN DREW HIS MEN to a point in the wood where he could watch the road leading to the East gate. Over their greenwood dress, each man had thrown a rough mantle making him look not unlike a friar.

"Look, master," quoth one of the widow's sons. "There comes a palmer along the road from the town. He can tell us if Stutely be in jeopardy."

"Go," answered Robin.

So Stout Will went out from the band while the others hid themselves and waited. When he had come close to the palmer he said, "I crave your pardon, but can you tell me tidings of Nottingham town? Do they intend to put an outlaw to death this day?"

"Yes," answered the palmer sadly.

"Who will shrive the poor wretch?" Stout Will asked reproachfully.

"Do you think that I should undertake this holy office?" asked the palmer.

"I do indeed!"

So the palmer was brought before Robin Hood, to whom he told all he knew of the situation. The men marched quickly until they were near to the western gate. Then Arthur-a-Bland quietly made his way to a point under the tower by the gate. Swinging himself up boldly by means of a friendly vine, he crept through the window and sprung upon the warden from behind. The warden soon lay bound and gagged upon the floor while Arthur-a-Bland slipped himself into his uniform and got hold of his keys.

'Twas the work of but a few moments to admit the band.

Presently, out came Will Stutely with firm step but dejected air. He was pushed into the cart which was to bear him to the gallows. But at this moment, a boyish-looking palmer stepped forth, and said:

"Your Excellency, let me at least shrive this poor wretch's soul."

The Bishop hesitated. He said a few words to the Sheriff, and the latter nodded to the monk ungraciously.

The palmer began to speak in a low voice to the condemned man. Then came another stir in the crowd and one came pushing through the press of people and soldiery to come near to the scaffold.

"Will, before you die, take leave of all your friends!" cried out Much, the miller's son. And with one stroke of his hunting knife he cut the bonds which fastened the prisoner's arms, and Stutely leaped lightly from the cart.

Shafts began to hurtle through the air, and Robin and his men cast aside their cloaks and sprang forward. The outlaws made good their lead and soon got through the gate and over the bridge. Close upon their heels came the soldiers.

The road leading to the forest was long and almost unprotected. But the outlaws retreated stubbornly. Stutely was in their midst, and the little palmer was there also.

Robin put his horn to his lips to sound a rally when a flying arrow from the enemy pierced his hand. The Sheriff gave a great huzza.

"Ha! You will shoot no more bows for a season, master outlaw!" he shouted.

"You lie!" retorted Robin fiercely, and he fitted the arrow which had wounded him and let it fly toward the Sheriff's head. The sharp point laid bare a deep gash upon the Sheriff's scalp and would certainly have killed him if it had come closer.

The palmer had whipped out a small white handkerchief and tried to staunch Robin's wound.

"Marian!" exclaimed Robin.

"I had to come, Robin," she said simply, "and I knew you would not let me."

Then from out of a gray castle poured a troop of men armed with pikes and axes. Robin recognized among the foremost of those coming from the castle, Sir Richard of the Lea. With a great cheer the outlaws raced up the hill and soon the whole force had gained the shelter of the castle. *Clash!* went one great door upon the other as they shut in the outlaw band, and shut out the Sheriff.

How Sir Richard Of The Lea Repaid His Debt

THE SHERIFF, AFTER LINGERING A FEW MOMENTS, was forced to withdraw. Meanwhile, Sir Richard had gone to Robin Hood and the two men greeted each other right gladly.

That night the foresters tarried within the friendly walls and the next day took leave; Sir Richard took Robin aside to his strong room and pressed him to take the four hundred golden pounds.

"Keep the money, for it is your own," said Robin.

Sir Richard's fair lady came forward and gave each yeoman a bow and a sheaf.

"These are poor presents," said Sir Richard. "But they carry with them a thousand times their weight in gratitude."

Meanwhile, the Sheriff went to inform the King. His Majesty had but lately returned from the crusades. The Sheriff spoke at length concerning Robin Hood and the traitorous knight Sir Richard of the Lea.

A fortnight later the King rode to Lea Castle. The King turned upon the knight and inquired: "What is this I hear about your castle's becoming a harbor for outlaws?"

Sir Richard of the Lea made a clean breast of how the outlaws had befriended him in sore need and how that he had given them only knightly protection in return.

The King liked the story well. "I must see this bold fellow for myself!" cried King Richard.

How King Richard Came
To Sherwood Forest

FRIAR TUCK HAD NURSED LITTLE JOHN'S wounded knee so skillfully that it was now healed. At last he took his leave, and he and the friar went forth to join the rest of the band. They sat around a big fire in great content.

A cold rain set in but the friar wended his way back to his little hermitage. He had sat himself down before a tankard of hot mulled wine and a pasty when suddenly a voice was heard on the outside demanding admission.

"A murrain seize you for disturbing a holy man in his prayers!" muttered Tuck savagely. He strode forth to see who his visitor might be.

The figure of a tall knight clad in a black coat of mail with plumed helmet stood before him.

"Have you no supper, brother?" asked the Black Knight

curtly. "I must e'en force my company upon you." And without further parley, the knight boldly strode past Tuck and entered the hermitage.

"Sit you down, Sir Knight," quoth he. "Half of my bed and board is yours this night."

The knight put aside the visor which had hid his face. He was a bearded man with blue eyes and hair shot with gold. The wine and warmth of the room cheered them both, and they were soon laughing uproariously as the best of comrades in the world. The two fell asleep together, one on each side of the table which had been cleared to the platters.

In the morning, they went their way into the forest. They had not proceeded more than three or four miles when all of a sudden the bushes just ahead of them parted and a well-knit man with curling brown hair stepped into the road. It was Robin Hood. Tuck, however, feigned not to know him at all.

"Hold!" cried Robin.

"Who is it bids me hold?" asked the knight quietly. "I am not in the habit of yielding to one man."

"Then here are others to keep me company," said Robin clapping his hands. And instantly a half-score other stalwart fellows came out of the bushes and stood beside him.

"We be yeomen of the forest, Sir Knight," continued Robin. "We have no means of support. We beseech ye to give us some of your spending."

The Black Knight now spoke again. "I am a messenger of the King," quoth he.

"God save the King!" said Robin, doffing his cap loyally. "I am Robin Hood! The King has no more devoted subject than I. I am glad that I have met you here. Be my friend and taste of our greenwood cheer."

"Gramercy!" replied the other smiling. "And now lead on to your greenwood hostelry."

So Robin went on the one side of the knight's steed, and Friar Tuck on the other, and the men went till they came to the open glade before the caves of Barnesdale. Then Robin drew forth his bugle and winded the three signal blasts of the band.

At the signal from Robin the dinner began. There was venison and fowl and fish and wheaten cake and ale and red wine in great plenty.

A horn winded in the glade, and a party of knights were seen approaching.

"'Tis Sir Richard of the Lea!" cried another, as the troop came nearer.

And so it was. Sir Richard dashed up to the camp. When he had come near the spot where the Black Knight stood he dismounted and knelt before him. "I trust Your Majesty has not needed our arms before," he said humbly.

"It is the King!" cried Will Scarlet, falling upon his knees.

"The King!" echoed Robin Hood after a moment of dumb wonderment, and he and all his men bent reverently upon their knees.

How Robin Hood
And Maid Marian Were Wed

RICHARD OF THE LION HEART looked over the kneeling band. "Swear!" he said in his full rich voice. "Swear that you, Robin Hood, and all your men from this day henceforth will serve the King!"

"We swear!" came once more the answering shout from the yeomen.

"Arise, then," said King Richard. "I give you all free pardon. I now appoint you to be Royal Archers. The half of your number shall come back to these woodlands as Royal Foresters. Where, now, is Little John?"

"Here, sire," quoth the giant, doffing his cap.

"Good master Little John," said the King, looking him over approvingly. You are this day Sheriff of Nottingham. I trust you will make a better official than the man you relieve."

"I shall do my best, sire," said Little John, with great astonishment and gladness in his heart.

"Master Scarlet," said the King, "I have heard of your tale. Accept the royal pardon and resume the care of your family estates."

Likewise the King called for Will Stutely and made him Chief of the Royal Archers. Then he summoned Friar Tuck to draw near.

"So what can I do for you in payment of last night's hospitality?" he asked.

"My lord," replied Tuck. "I wish only for peace in this life."

Richard sighed. "You ask the greatest thing in the world,

brother—contentment." He glanced around once more at the foresters. "Which one of you is Allan-a-Dale?" he asked, and Allan came forward. "So," said the King with sober face. "You are that errant minstrel who stole a bride at Plympton. Now what excuse have you to make?"

"Only that I loved her, sire, and she loved me," said Allan, simply, "and the Norman lord would have married her because of her lands."

"From tomorrow you and Mistress Dale are to return to them and live in peace and loyalty." He continued, turning to Robin Hood, "did you not have a sweetheart—one Mistress Marian? What has become of her, that you should have forgotten her?"

"Nay, Your Majesty," said the black-eyed page coming forward. "Robin has not forgotten me!"

"So!" said the King, bending to kiss her small hand. "Are you not the only child of the late Earl of Huntingdon?"

"I am, sire. However, the estates are confiscate."

"Then they shall be restored forthwith!" cried the King." I bestow them upon you jointly. Come forward, Robin Hood."

Robin came and knelt before his king. Richard drew his sword and touched him upon the shoulder. "Rise, Robin Fitzooth, Earl of Huntingdon!" he exclaimed, while a mighty cheer arose from the band. "The first command I give you, my lord Earl, is to marry Mistress Marian without delay."

"May I obey all Your Majesty's commands as willingly!" cried the new Earl of Huntingdon. "The ceremony shall take place tomorrow."

Then the King chatted with others of the foresters and made himself as one of them for the evening. 'Twas a happy, carefree night—this last one together under the greenwood tree.

In the morning, the company was early astir and on their way to Nottingham. Almost before the company had crossed the moat the news spread through the town like wildfire.

"The King is here! The King is here and hath taken Robin Hood!"

From every corner flocked the people to cheer for the King, who rode down through the marketplace. At the far end of it, he was met by the Sheriff who came up puffing in his haste to do the King honor.

"Sir Sheriff," quoth the King, "I have determined to place in charge of this shire a man who fears no other man in it, Master Little John. You will turn over the keys to him forthwith."

The Sheriff bowed but dared utter no word. Then the King turned to the Bishop of Hereford who had also come up to pay his respects.

"This afternoon you must officiate at the wedding of two of our company in Nottingham Church. So make you ready."

The company then rode on to the Mansion House, where the whole town made a holiday.

In the afternoon, the way from the Mansion House to Nottingham Church was lined with cheering people as the wedding party passed by. The service was said in Latin, while the organ pealed forth softly. Then the happy party dispersed and Robin and Marian passed out again through the portal, man and wife.

And thus, the new Earl of Huntingdon and his bride began
their wedded life.

How Robin Hood
Met His Death

THE ROYAL ARCHERS WERE DIVIDED into two bands.
One-half of them were retained in London, while the other
half returned to Sherwood to guard the King's preserves.

Several months passed by and Robin began to chafe under
the restraint of city life. Finally he became so distraught that he
asked leave to travel in foreign lands. He took Marian with him,
and in an Eastern land Marian sickened of a plague and died.

Robin came back to the court at London but Richard
was gone again upon his adventures and Prince John acted as
Regent. The Prince bade his guards seize Robin and cast him
into the Tower.

He was released by the faithful Stutely and the remnant
of the Royal Archers. All together they fled the city and made
their way to the greenwood. One and all lived quietly
with Robin.

The news came that King Richard had met his death in
a foreign land and John reigned as King in his stead. The new
King waged fierce war upon the outlaws.

In one of the sorties Robin was wounded. The cut did not
seem serious, but it left a lurking fever. One day as he rode along
on horseback near Kirklees Abbey, Robin was seized with a rush
of blood to the head. He dismounted weakly and knocked at the

Abbey gate. A woman shrouded in black peered forth.

At the name of Robin Hood the woman unbarred the door and admitted him. Then she spoke hurriedly in a low voice: "Your fever will sink if you are bled." So she bled him, and he fell into a stupor.

Now there is a dispute as to this abbess who bled him. Some say that she was none other than the former Sheriff's daughter.

Robin's eyes swam from very weakness when he awoke. He set his horn unto his mouth and blew out three weak blasts. Little John was out in the forest near by. He made haste and came running up to the door of the abbey. He burst in the door and soon came running up to the room where Robin lay.

"Lift me up, good Little John," Robin said brokenly. "Give me my good yew bow and fix a broad arrow upon the string. Out yonder where this arrow shall fall let them dig my grave."

And he sped his shaft out of the open window till it dropped in the shadow of the trees. Then he fell back upon the breast of his devoted friend. So died the body of Robin Hood, but his spirit lives on in the hearts of men who love freedom and chivalry.